1 ZANY ZOO

By
Lori Degman

Illustrated by
Colin Jack

WINNER!
Cheerios®
NEW AUTHOR
CONTEST

9:00

SIMON & SCHUSTER BOOKS FOR YOUNG READERS
NEW YORK   LONDON   TORONTO   SYDNEY

To my mother, for raising me
in a wonderfully zany zoo,
and to John, Sean, and Brian,
for helping me keep the tradition going—L. D.

To Michelle Jack—C. J.

The author thanks the Cheerios® Spoonfuls of Stories® judges for
choosing 1 Zany Zoo and the 3 J's for making this an incredible experience!

SIMON & SCHUSTER BOOKS FOR YOUNG READERS · An imprint of Simon &
Schuster Children's Publishing Division · 1230 Avenue of the Americas, New
York, New York 10020 · Text copyright © 2010 by Lori Degman · Illustrations
copyright © 2010 by Colin Jack · All rights reserved, including the right of
reproduction in whole or in part in any form. · SIMON & SCHUSTER BOOKS FOR YOUNG READERS
is a trademark of Simon & Schuster, Inc. · For information about special discounts for
bulk purchases, please contact Simon & Schuster Special Sales at 1-866-506-1949
or business@simonandschuster.com. · The Simon & Schuster Speakers Bureau can
bring authors to your live event. For more information or to book an event, contact
the Simon & Schuster Speakers Bureau at 1-866-248-3049 or visit our website at
www.simonspeakers.com. · Book design by Chloë Foglia · The text for this book is
set in Coop. · The illustrations for this book are rendered digitally. · Manufactured in
China · 1010 PXA · 10 9 8 7 6 5 4 3 2 · Library of Congress Cataloging-in-Publication
Data · Degman, Lori. · 1 zany zoo / Lori Degman ; illustrated by Colin Jack. – 1st ed.
· p. cm. · Summary: When one fearless fox grabs the zookeeper's keys and opens
all the cages, increasing numbers of animals behave in most unusual ways. ·
ISBN 978-1-4169-8990-5 (hardcover) · [1. Stories in rhyme. 2. Zoo animals–Fiction.
3. Counting.] I. Jack, Colin, ill. II. Title. III. Title: One zany zoo. · PZ8.3.D3642Aac 2010 ·
[E]–dc22 · 2009003776

While YOU stood here waiting, with nothing to do,
I snuck through the gate and into the zoo.
You'll never believe what I saw—what I heard.
I swear it's the truth—every last word.

While YOU stood here waiting, with nothing to do,
I snuck through the gate and into the zoo.
You'll never believe what I saw—what I heard.
I swear it's the truth—every last word.

1 fearless fox grabbed the zookeeper's keys.
He used them to set all the animals free.

The zookeeper chased him, but fox kept his cool
and—splash!—landed right in the walrus's pool.

2 sporty zebras in goggles and flippers
were snipping the walrus's whiskers with clippers.
One did the combing, the other the trimming.
They swept up the clippings, then all four went swimming.

3 fussy beavers cooked chili for lunch.
They also baked cornbread and mixed a fruit punch.
They seasoned and tasted till each one agreed,
then called "Come and get it!" and caused a stampede.

4 anxious elephants packed up their trunks,
to flee from their neighbors—a family of skunks.
They tried wearing clothespins to block out the smell,
but that didn't help, so they bid them farewell.

5 clever chimps waited high in the trees
and watched as the zookeeper searched for his keys.

He peeked behind bushes
and underneath rocks,

and when he gave up,
they high-fived the fox.

I tried to imagine what else they had planned.
Then somebody hollered,

6 groovy 'roos tapped the beat with their shoes,
and laughing hyenas sang rhythm and blues.
A lizard in sunglasses wailed on the sax,
while monkeys kept time on the box turtles' backs.

7 sad hippos were making repairs,
from damage they caused playing musical chairs.

The music stopped playing; they scrambled to sit.

Didn't they know they were too big to fit?

8 pompous peacocks were proud as can be
while strutting their stuff for the whole zoo to see.
They primped and they preened to get just the right looks,
as fans gathered round holding autograph books.

9 fickle leopards were waiting in line
to trade in their spots for some fresh new designs.
They chose among triangles, diamonds, or squares,
rectangles, ovals, or star shapes to wear.

10 rowdy bears led a big zoo parade.
The animals modeled the costumes they'd made.
They waved to the crowd from the traveling stages.

The zookeeper shouted,

He locked the last cage at a minute to nine.

He tossed me outside and said, "Get back in line!"

It may sound outrageous, but one thing is true,
when nobody's looking, that's 1 zany zoo!